Suppose You Meet a DiNOSAUR

A First Book of Manners

Suppose You Meet a

DiNOSAUR

A First Book of Manners

by JUDY SIERRA
illustrated by TIM BOWERS

DRAGONFLY BOOKS
New York

You're shopping at the grocery store.
Surprise!
You see a dinosaur.
This doesn't happen every day.
So, what are you supposed to say?

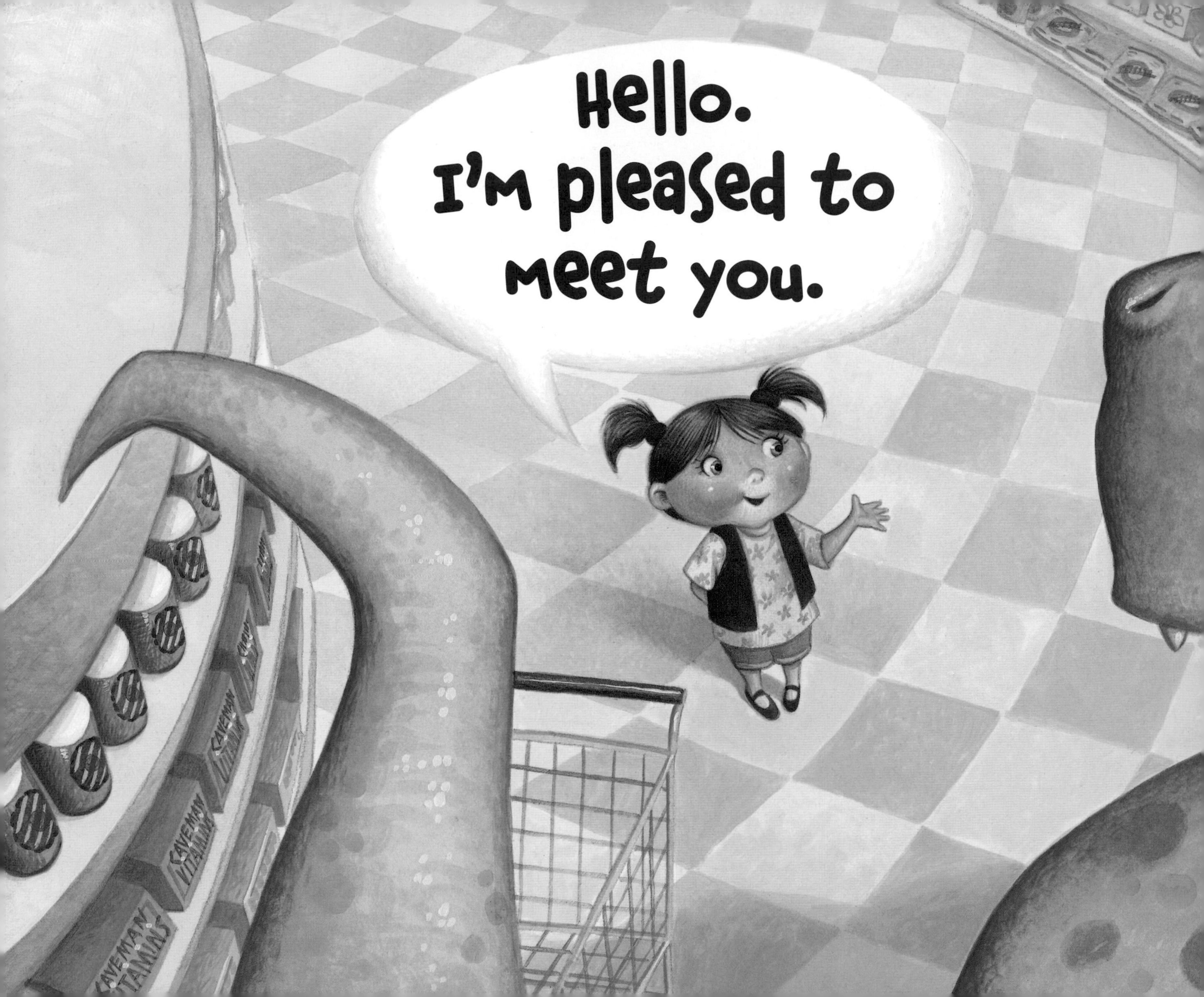
Hello.
I'm pleased to
meet you.
CAVEMAN VITAMINS

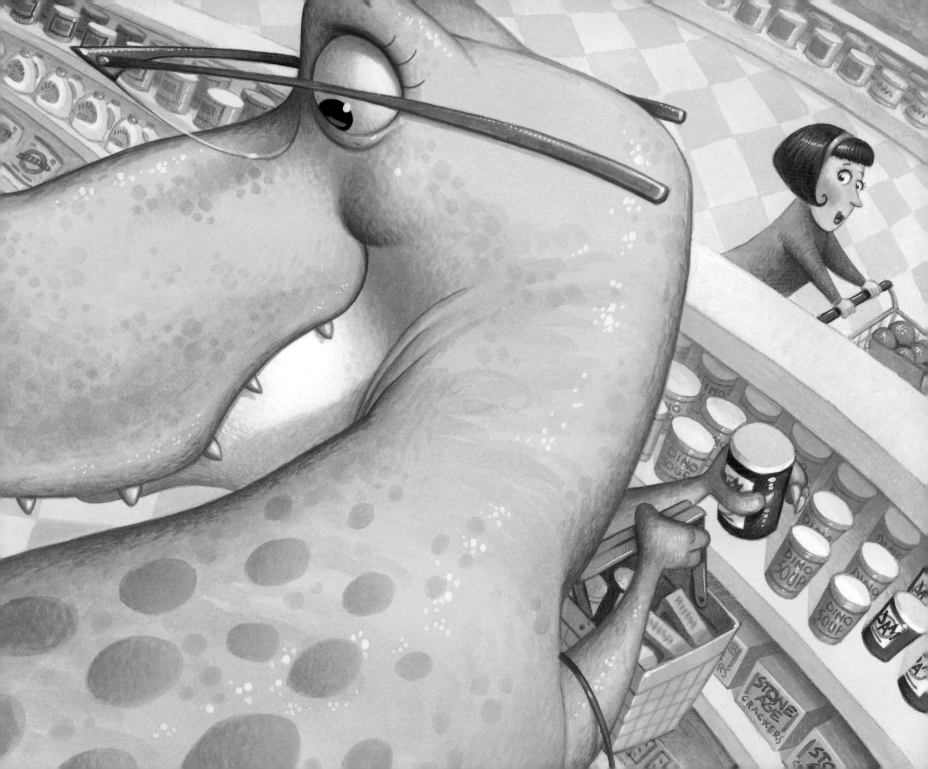

Imagine that the dinosaur
Is standing by a bathroom door.
You have to pee! She's in your way.
Quick! What's the proper thing to say?

Commotion in the produce aisle!
The dinosaur upsets a pile
Of apples, and they roll away.
If you pick them up, what will **she** say?

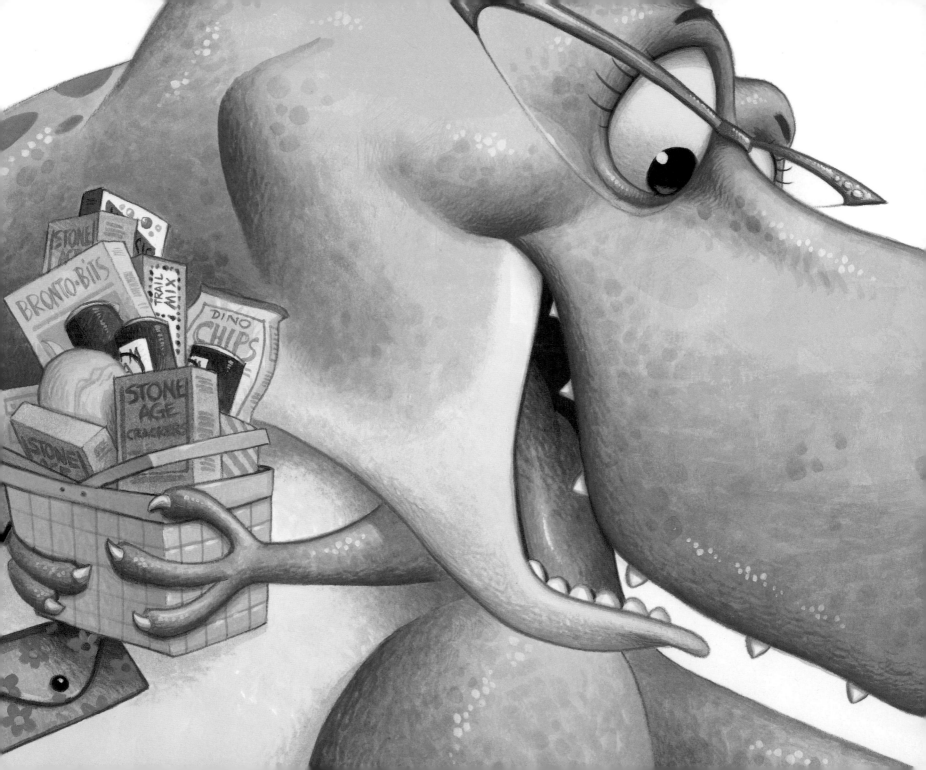

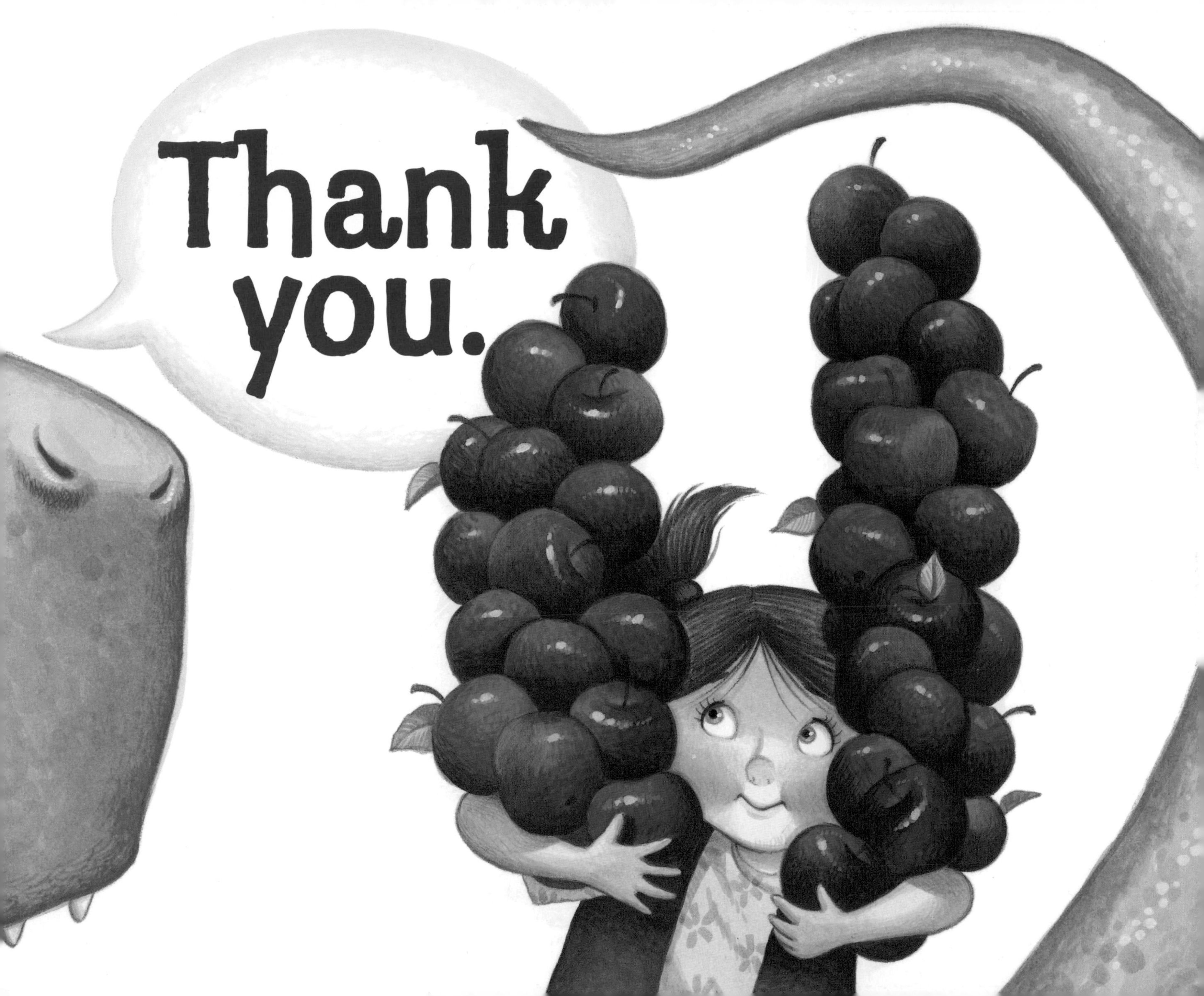
Thank you.

Your shopping cart begins to spin.
It dings the dino on the shin.
She roars a terrifying roar.
What do you tell the dinosaur?

The dinosaur then gives you four
Banana chips (which you adore).
She asks you, "Would you like some more?"
How do you answer the dinosaur?

You want to buy some butter brickle.
Yikes! You need another nickel.
The dinosaur says, "Here's a dime."
What are the magic words this time?

Thank you.
Here's your change.
Would you like some
butter brickle?
Judy's
Butter Brickle

The dinosaur cannot eat brickle.
Brickle makes her tonsils tickle.
She doesn't want it, even slightly.
How does she let you know politely?

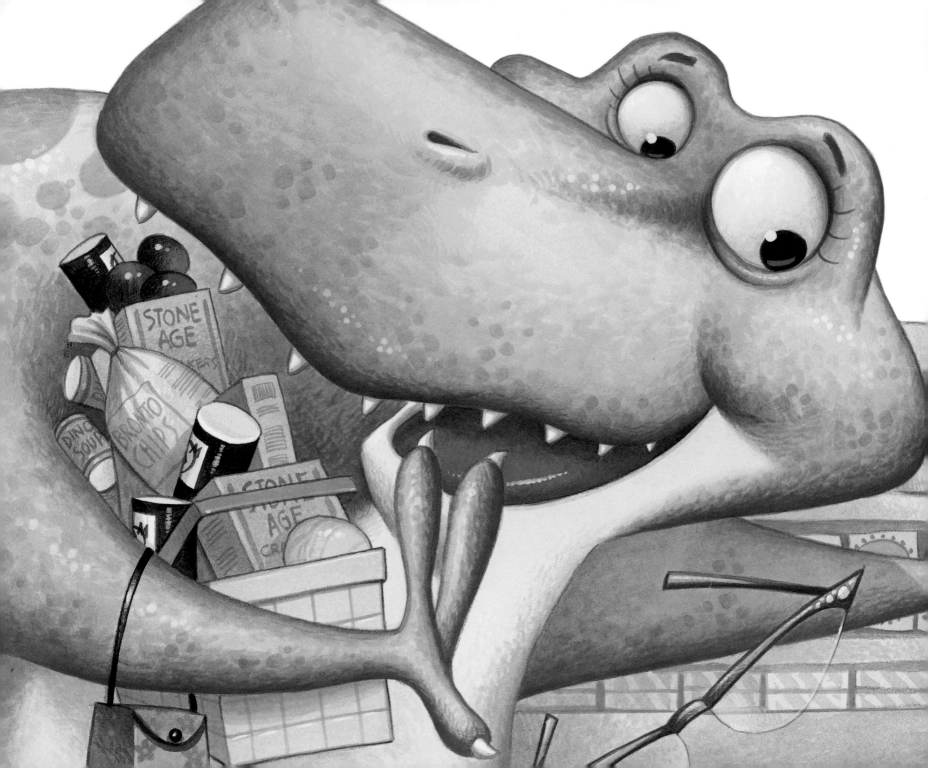

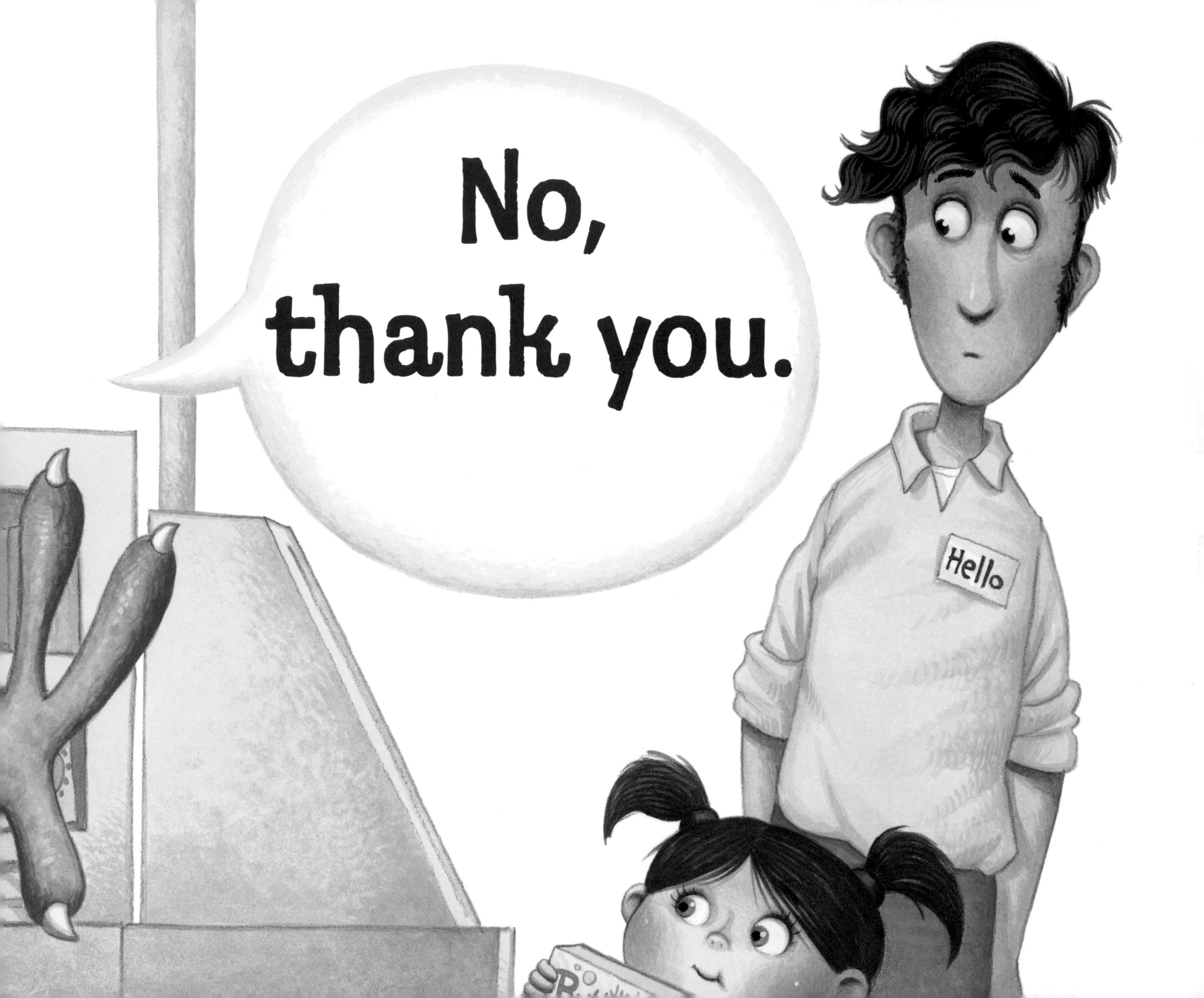
No, thank you.
Hello

You find her glasses on the floor
And hand them to the dinosaur.
She smiles and says,
"Why, thank you, dear."
What words does she
    expect to hear?

Out the door of the grocery store
Tromps the friendly dinosaur.
She's waving as she drives away.
I'm sure you know the words to say.

Goodbye.
It was nice to meet you.

All rights reserved. Published in the United States by Dragonfly Books, an imprint of Random House Children's Books,
a division of Penguin Random House LLC, New York. Originally published in hardcover in the United States by Alfred A. Knopf,
an imprint of Random House Children's Books, New York, in 2012.

Dragonfly Books with the colophon is a registered trademark of Penguin Random House LLC.

Visit us on the Web! rhcbooks.com

Educators and librarians, for a variety of teaching tools, visit us at RHTeachersLibrarians.com

The Library of Congress has cataloged the hardcover edition of this work as follows:
Sierra, Judy.
Suppose you meet a dinosaur : a first book of manners / by Judy Sierra ; illustrated by Tim Bowers. — 1st ed.
p.   cm.
Summary: Illustrates basic polite behavior that one might need to use while grocery shopping at the same time as a dinosaur.
ISBN 978-0-375-86720-0 (trade) — ISBN 978-0-375-96720-7 (lib. bdg.) — ISBN 978-0-375-98729-8 (ebook)
[1. Courtesy—Fiction. 2. Grocery shopping– Fiction. 3. Dinosaurs—Fiction] I. Bowers, Tim, ill. II. Title.
PZ83.S577Sup 2012
[E]—dc22
2009037576

ISBN 978-1-101-93250-6 (pbk.)

MANUFACTURED IN MALAYSIA
10 9 8 7 6 5

First Dragonfly Books Edition

FOR JANET SCHULMAN

Suppose you meet an editor
Who mixes words and art.
To make books fun for everyone,
She plays a magic part.

For when you go to turn the page
And then you stop and smile,
You linger and you look again,
As Janet whispers, "Stay awhile."

Thank you, Janet.